Nasima H. Khan has been a career journalist—a writer and editor in the print media in New Delhi, India, and later in Muscat, Oman. A Wolfson Press Fellow of Cambridge University, UK, she thereafter turned to teaching journalism and communication at a college of the Ministry of Higher Education, Oman. She now lives in India, in the suburbs of New Delhi.

To my amazing boys, who have brought sunshine
and laughter into my life

Nasima H. Khan

FADING TALES OF THE DECCAN

AUSTIN MACAULEY PUBLISHERS™
LONDON • CAMBRIDGE • NEW YORK • SHARJAH

ISBN 9789948771234 (Paperback)
ISBN 9789948771227 (E-Book)

Application Number: MC-10-01-4016775
Age Classification: E

Printer Name: iPrint Global Ltd
Printer Address: Witchford, England

First Published 2024
AUSTIN MACAULEY PUBLISHERS FZE
Sharjah Publishing City
P.O Box [519201]
Sharjah, UAE
www.austinmacauley.ae
+971 655 95 202

Table of Content

Preface

Throughout my childhood, I have seen women around me who have led their lives with a sense of purpose, regulating their daily routines to consider each member of their rather large households. They handled their relations with kindness, patience and grace, never leaving out a single member of their families. They tirelessly supported every endeavor of their menfolk, wholeheartedly plunging themselves into the services required of them in order to make a success of their husbands' and sons' plans, always with a smile on their faces. These remarkable women never thought to ask for recognition or praise.

After a busy day catering to the many needs of their families, they would gather in the evenings, seeking out a cool breeze, and together would weave chains of white jasmine and moghra with which they would adorn and perfume the hair of each woman in that company. For them, it was a small daily pleasure.

Such was the generation of my mother, grandmothers, aunts, their cousins and so on. It is they who would exchange jokes, and rhymes, and stories – handed down to them through an oral tradition from the women of the family before them. They would also enchant the younger children through this tradition of sharing stories, telling them repeatedly and always finding laughter. These traditions kept strong the bond between these women, who were so protected and secluded within the walls of their dwellings. They knew only the life they lived and little else beyond. They did not understand the value of their selflessness and did not know to ask for more. It is these women who have left a deep imprint on women of my generation.

The Fading Tales of the Deccan is a tribute to these unsung women and is a retelling of the stories they shared over generations. Stories told in the oral tradition can rarely keep their form. They are stripped down by one teller and embellished by another. A twist is added by one and a turn by another. It is hard to say what their original form was, but these stories are certainly inspired by nature, by the life lived in pre-modern India, and not surprisingly, by women. Recalled from an era gone by, these tales have been reconstructed to appeal to the modern-day child as they tell of a world that once existed and which children of the future may never likely know.

I would like to thank my marvelous parents for their love and guidance and our exciting travels, which have unfurled to me a glorious view of the world. Thanks also to my wonderful husband who champions all that I do, with patience and constant encouragement.

Introduction

Away from busy school schedules and into semi-rural expanses with fresh air and loads of cousins and other children, summer vacations at grandparents' place is perhaps the most charming phase of growing up. A child hears from her grandmother, tales handed down through generations. She meets and learns from others of her age-group, charming chants and age-old games that have all but disappeared from city life.

Stories and rhymes that one hears in childhood somehow continue to live on in the mind throughout the seasons of life and into one's golden years. The words don't always make sense but their measure continues to flow beneath conscious thought, dwelling in a place of happiness. Their charm lingers in memories of bygone moments of laughter with siblings, of pranks hatched with playmates, in happy chants or even baiting taunts of childhood friends and foes.

A little late in life, I found myself trying to make sense of a garbled basket of words that I would play-chant as a child visiting cousins, aunts and uncles scattered across the Deccan plateau of peninsular India. Our chants were uttered in a local dialect of the Urdu language, called Deccani Urdu (also Dakhni Urdu). Sometimes, a sprinkle of Telugu words would find their way into the rhymes. As I tried to make sense of what I remember, I have rediscovered a virtual treasure of tales and rhymes of an era gone by, which children of the modern age could probably not imagine.

In this work, I have reconstructed some almost-forgotten stories and attempted to make sense of charming childhood chants so unfamiliar to the modern-day child, and I had immense fun doing so. All of the tales here are narrated by a spreading peepal tree (*Ficus religiosa*), which has seen the passage of time on the bank of an unnamed river in an unnamed town. I would recommend that parents read these tales aloud to their children so the entire family may enjoy them together.

Chapter 1
The Great Peepal Tree

Gather around my little ones. Come together under my shade.

Sisters! Stop your quarrel this instance! There is much you need to learn, and one important lesson is never to quarrel. Deepa, you say you are not quarreling? Why so noisy, then? And Leena, don't blame your sister. Stop! Quiet! If I could frown, I would frown at you. But I can only shed some leaves on you and remain silent until you settle down like good children. Pinky, you too.

And now you giggle! I know Pinky is a boy.

Ah! Finally you have settled down. So listen now, children, I am the Great Peepal tree. Listen to the rustle of my leaves and the many songs they sing, the many tales they tell. There is much wisdom in the stories of yesteryears, and perhaps you will imbibe some lessons from them that will stand you in good stead far into your future. Gather some of my wisdom earned from long years of standing here, rooted in this very place. And gather some of my older, thick-veined leaves for there are some wonderful crafts you can make with them later, at your leisure.

My tales are from a time long ago, when I was as large and spreading as I am now, but not quite as advanced in years.

My leaves were always a happy green, heart shaped with an extended tip, each one fluttering in the breeze to its own tune. Yes, mine is an important family, some of us bearing small figs, and others possessing medicinal properties to which humans have turned for centuries. It was under the branches of the Bodhi tree of our family that the Lord Buddha found enlightenment. But I did not exist then. So I will not talk of that. I will talk about this town and the time that I know of – a time when people used to live almost the way you do, but there were no air conditioners.

You look surprised. Yes, only trees such as I offered people shade from the heat and allowed the breeze to blow through our leaves. Under our branches, people would come together, seeking out the coolness of our shade in the hot sun. They would talk, joke, laugh, gossip, conduct business and sometimes even disagree with each other. But being polite and respectful was highly valued. There were no technology toys to distract them, no screens such as those that engage you at home now, so engrossing that your mothers tire of seeing you sitting around and order you outside to get some sunshine and play.

Once, children used to come outside because they wanted to. In our branches, they would tie swings of thick coir ropes and wooden boards and later on, from discarded car tires. They would soar back and forth screaming with delight or play with their friends with pebbles, cowrie shells, pretty glass marbles and with bicycle tires, running them with a stick to keep balance. That was a different time when there were no tarred roads as you see today, and no cars – not even the ancient Ambassador. What is that? Well, you will have to ask your grandfather.

Do you see those chirping sparrows? There used to be many of them in the old times. A woman, like your mother, would bring a winnowing basket outside her house there – just there – to clean the rice of impurities. The sparrows would noisily hop about her feet waiting for her to throw a handful of broken rice their way. Sometimes, she would balance a child on her hip as she did her household chores. Even a crying baby would bounce with laughter when she would call to the sparrow.

Call to the Sparrow

Churdi, churdi aa;
Dana khaa, paani pee,
Brrrrr urdh ke jaa!

Whatever does that mean? Oh, child, let me explain:

Little birdie, hi!
Come down, don't be shy.
Drink and feed, on drops and seed.
Brrrr, away you fly!

Yes, they would laugh just as you are laughing now.

Their fathers napped near my trunk. Mothers chatted there, at the edge of my shade towards the East where my shadow would lengthen with evening, and children like you would sit nearby and splay their fingers and chant till each one was counted out and one finger won. The chant:

A Mixed Basket

Agla magla naas karela
Auni ki dauni ki jab ka pada
Seedhe hath ka navva nada
Aam, jam, chikni matthi tham!

This and that… a bitter brown gourd,
A shawl… or a scarf, to use as you would,
A clean pajama chord the right hand can tie,
A mango, a guava… get a grip, smooth guy!

They would play a similar game of counting their toes while
calling out for their brother:

Brother from Afar

Bhai ba'door, bhai ba'door!
Ab jayengey kitni door?
Naddi aayee bharpoor!
Hathiyan dubaiyenge,
Ghode thairayengey…
Amili ke pedh ke neechey
Hum se milo bhai! Char koni chai!
Jungle-jungle mhendi piki,
Bhai ka paun ghulam!

You want to know what it means, of course, but I can only
guess. Maybe, it happened in the monsoon season when rivers
would swell with rain. If it means anything at all, it would be:

Brother from afar; oh, brother from afar!
What distance need we go?
The river is brimming over
and our elephants would drown slow,
although our horses could swim…

Better we meet, brother dear,
under the tamarind tree,
where our foursquare game
could include six, to our glee!
In every jungle, the henna bush grows;
Little choice have you Brother, only woes,
For in our hue will we color your toes!

As for the rhyme that talks of punishing naughty children:

Appadi ki thappadi, pakeley paan,
Udh gayi chidiya, pakardo kaan!

And so I tell you 'girls, do not quarrel'. Or else,

Dough rounds slapped from palm to palm,
If they were cheeks, they'd burn red
The bird has flown, the quarrel's gone,
So touch your ears and make amends!

Chapter 2
Summer: June

I have much to tell you, my little ones. I, a mighty peepal tree, have tasted the soil of your ancestors. My great trunk has stood strong through the ups and downs of history and withstood the changing landscape. My strong branches have borne witness to many a deed, good and bad. My clever leaves have heard the music in the wind and the words that travel on the air from afar. Their veins thickened with this knowledge, they deposit their tales with me before falling off and making way for bright new leaves to dance in the breeze and tell me more about the changing times.

So yes, I have many a charming chant for you pretty little Pinky, and you my happy Leena of the big smile and of course for you, wise Deepa, who I know will repeat and remind your sister and brother of the stories I tell. But now, listen to this tale from a hot summer day. It is a tale so terrifying that your forefathers could never forget it, no matter how hard they shook their heads. Yet, children of that time entrapped it into enchanting words, which I will relate to you at the end of this telling.

It was mid-morning on a hot summer's day. Elsewhere, far up in the mountains, it had rained, filling up the stream that ran through a gorge with the town set high on both sides. If you look down east, you can still see the stream, though it is but a trickle now. You can still see the town, but it is big and crowded now with far fewer trees. And all that garbage that you see dumped in so many places alongside what used to be the stream? Well, there was no garbage like that back then.

Impossible, you say! It was possible then. All household waste was recyclable. There were no plastics. But getting back to our story…

Sitting high in her carriage drawn by two white horses, a pale lady looked haughtily down at the townspeople scurrying about the busy market place. A delicate silken hand fan, a bonnet over her fair curls and a parasol above protected her from the sun and the heat. Her eyes were bluer than the sky of that hot, dusty day. A blush of pink in her flouncy cream dress made her a pretty picture. A pretty haughty picture, as she barely acknowledged the bowed greetings of the dark natives her carriage rode past.

Natives? Well, that is what the British colonial rulers once called us Indians. Even me – they called me a 'native neem' even though I am a peepal!

A young, eager coachman quickly steered the pale lady's carriage towards the single, narrow, wooden bridge in the town. The stream below was swelled, rushing with the run-off of plentiful rainfall in the hills. There was just enough room on the bridge for the carriage to pass. The townsfolk on foot there, squeezed to the sides of the bridge with no grumble or display of inconvenience. The lady's eyes were set on the horizon where the hills were covered with lush green forests.

Yes, yes, those very hills out there, which are now brown and spew dust devils into the hot air that carries into town when there is a wind from the west. Oh, so dusty, masking my bright green leaves until the monsoon comes and washes it away. But getting back to the story…

Midway on the bridge, the carriage stopped. The pale lady dragged her wistful eyes away from the cool deep-green distance and looked about her, a frown beginning to mar her face at the scene ahead.

In a palanquin, borne on the broad shoulders of four sturdy men, sat the beautiful wife of an eminent merchant. Bright jewels sparkled against her dusky, luminescent skin at the window of her conveyance. "Brothers, why have you stopped," her musical voice demanded of her litter-bearers.

"There is a madam in her carriage blocking the way," replied the lead-bearer, describing to her what she could already view.

"Tell that coachman to go back," she commanded with a scornful glance at the pale lady. Her tone brooked no argument. Clearly, she was used to being obeyed.

The bearer conveyed the same, and the coachman obediently began to back the carriage and horses off the bridge.

Stung by the palanquin rider's evident scorn, anger stirred in the pale lady's heart. "What do you think you are doing?" she demanded of her coachman. "Have you gone mad? We cannot go back. They have to!"

Sweating profusely in terror, the trembling coachman conveyed the English command to the palanquin bearer, who in turn conversed with his mistress.

Feminine haughtiness ran high on both sides. The physical discomfort caused by the heat of the day further frayed tempers. Excited townsfolk gathered around, gaping stupidly at the stand-off between the two most prominent women of the town – the magistrate's wife and that of the richest merchant of the district.

The coachman reigned in his horses in confusion. Seeing this as a sign of what they perceived a retreat, the palanquin bearers upped their pressure by arguing hotly with him. They knew their merchant master would whip them if he heard they had backed down on the bridge and allowed this great insult to his social status. Feeling the heat from both sides, the coachman was in tears. The pale lady behind him too was threatening him with a whipping for disobeying her…

The frightened coachman with tears streaming down his cheeks struggled to get the horses as far right as possible while the palanquin bearers steadily advanced in the opposite direction practically clinging to their side of the bridge.

In this moment of madness, the horses suddenly turned skittish. The ornate hub of the carriage wheel caught under the carved wooden base of the palanquin. In an instant, the palanquin tipped dangerously towards the river, with two bearers kicking the air before letting go and dropping to the road. The momentum caused the palanquin poles to roll off the broad shoulders of the other two bearers. There was no way anyone could prevent the palanquin along with its occupant tumbling over the side of the bridge, straight into the swirling waters below. It took but a second.

The bearers and several swimmers jumped into the river in a bid to rescue the merchant's wife. As they dragged her limp form to the shore, there was blood everywhere from her cracked skull which had hit a boulder and from her swollen belly that could be seen by all.

The pale lady collapsed in her carriage. For once, the coachman took charge. Instinctively, he knew he had to get the lady out before the crowd reacted with anger. Tearful and sweating nervously, he hurriedly backed the carriage off the bridge, without heeding the people scurrying out of his path. Once on solid ground, he turned the horses around and raced them towards the magistrate's residence.

The pale lady was in silent shock. When they rumbled into the compound of the magistrate's bungalow, she was sans her parasol with her bonnet askew and her face bloodless. Angry townspeople chasing the carriage were only a few hundred yards behind them. Taking in the scene, the gatekeepers shut and barred the gates of the magistrate's residence as soon as the lady entered.

Outside, more angry townspeople gathered. Some had hitched up their *lungis* (checkered sarongs) and threateningly wielded thick bamboo staffs. Tempers ran high. Some more townspeople rode in on oxen-drawn carts – the oxen with their great horns shaking threateningly from side to side.

The magistrate, who was home, narrowed his eyes. The priority, he decided, was to protect his wife and also to ensure the safety of other English folk in this area. He clamped an immediate curfew on the town till further orders and sent for the police force to disperse the gathered townspeople. He also sent out guarded carriages to bring all English families to the magistrate's sprawling residence.

Why have I fallen silent you ask? Ah! I was recalling a moment akin to a miracle. A great gust of wind blew at that very moment and dust flew in every direction. It shook my branches wildly, causing my old leaves to shed. From high up in my branches, it unseated a crow that cawed disquietly. The dust storm sent the townspeople running for cover wherever they could find it. Most of them turned and headed home. The sky darkened and suddenly, rain began to fall in big drops. People began to run towards the town. In that one moment, the coming of the rain changed everything. It cooled tempers and changed priorities. The prospect of violence was washed away as people made their way back, their thoughts now on how to secure their homes, their families and granaries from the monsoon rain.

In the same moment, that rain soothed my shaken core. When the drenched police marched their horses in, only the bereaved merchant remained outside, inconsolable. His wife had died an unexpected and bloody death, taking their unborn child with her. The magistrate ruled the entire incident as an unfortunate accident with compensation to be paid to those affected.

Of course that was no justice for the merchant. He grieved for many months and eventually turned mad. His empire of riches collapsed. People shook their heads to forget. The oxen too shook their great horns. But they did not forget. They still shake their great horns from time to time when they remember the events of that bloody day. Every monsoon, my branches too shake wildly as the wind reminisces that untold tale. And in case I forget… see that crow over there? Yes, the one with the jarring caw. His caw-caw call reminds me of that tale all over again.

Sisters, never quarrel. It was not an accident that caused the death of the merchant's wife. It was the haughtiness of the two women that caused it. Their sense of self-importance, their lack of humility and their unwillingness to compromise took two lives.

Caw, caw it says! And yes, the crow has returned! All that remains of the tale is the chant you sometimes hear in his jarring song:

The Louse

Kaali june aati thi, Ujli june jaati thi.
Kaali june ka pet phuta, Nadima laal hui.
Bail ke singhan hiley, Jhaard ke patte jhardey.
Cawwa kar-kar. Baqaal deewana.

The dark louse came this way,
the bright louse went that way,
The dark louse's tummy bled
and mother river turned red.
The oxen shook their great horns,
the leaves of the peepal shed;
The crow cried kar-kar
and the grieving merchant lost his head.

Chapter 3
Monsoon: Saramma

Welcome children. Enjoy the cool breeze beneath my branches as the rain has let up. Seat yourselves on the low brick ledge that thoughtful men built around me so many years ago. It has protected me, ensuring no one encroaches on my root space. It has also drawn so many people to sit in my shade, enjoy the fresh air and sip a cup of tea.

Yes, take out your marbles. Even bring your board games. Maybe it's a little damp, but a little dampness never hurt anybody. Maybe it is a little green with moss, but that only makes it prettier. Don't say 'ew' to my little friends – the earthworms till the soil, keeping my roots fresh and well-tended. The toads feed on the irritating insects that crawl into my bark.

Well, yes, the crow still irritates me with his caw. But to be fair, he is not so bad. Look at that iridescent ring of blue-black feathers about his neck. Not quite as pretty as the rose ring about the green parakeet's neck or the spectacular yellow band of the golden oriole. So many birds roost in my branches. Hear the musical bulbuls, so smart in their black and white tuxedo-like plumage, the loud mynahs, the knock-knock of the woodpecker followed by its resounding call and the sleek black koyal with its splendid song… oh, so many birds. But my favorite remains the unassuming sparrow.

Remember? I told you about the sparrows that gathered at your mother's feet, and those of all the mothers who came before her. Your mother would linger until the birds finished feeding. If she stepped away, the sly crow would come and steal their meal, so she kept watch.

Yes, the sparrow is an endearing bird. Look how the male with its dark ringed eyes and a black tuft on its chin slants its neck in expectation. The black, brown and white of his feathers are so vibrant. The females are gentler in color and smaller – so easy to overlook or to underestimate.

Do you know the story of the sparrow and the crow? Come, hear it from me then. Hear about a tiny sparrow in the song of Saramma.

Song of Saramma

Saramma, the sparrow, toiled tireless through the day.
She gathered golden grain and stored it all away.
Morn after morn Saramma steadfast worked the field,
Filling up her storage urn with the summer's yield.

The monsoon clouds would herald only wind and rain;
No food for her babies – just misery and pain.
So thrifty Saramma stocked up and barred her door.
The monsoon winds raged and the sky began to pour.

Lightning danced, thunder clapped through the windy night.
Saramma crooned to calm her fledglings in their fright.

Howling wind, pouring rain – fearsome was their battle.
Suddenly, her dwelling's door did shiver and rattle.

"Saramma, Saramma, I am drenched, let me in.
Saramma, Saramma, it's me, Crow, your cousin!"
Saramma paled. A trickster at her door. Oh, shoo!.
"Go away Crow," she called. "I have no room for you."

"Sweet cousin, don't be cruel, Saramma, pretty dear.
I'll nap in your pantry; with dawn I'll fly, don't fear!"
No trust had Saramma in her smooth-talking kin,
Yet soft of heart, she pondered and finally let him in.

With a drip of thanks, Crow slipped into the pantry.
Saramma stayed alert so nothing would go awry.
The babies slept. She stayed awake, she yawned, she hopped.
Just as morning broke, her eyelids finally dropped.

Waking to a hungry brood making their demand,
She dipped into the urn, but no grain came to hand.
"Woe be me!" Saramma cried. "Crow fed and flew!"
He'd gorged on the grain and left an urn-full of goo!

The children giggled, then after a while fell silent. They
looked at each other, their discomfort rising. We have to go,
they said, and suddenly ran home. Whatever could be the
matter?

The children are back again so soon. What could the
matter be? They do not look happy.

"Great Peepal Tree," Deepa began, after the three of them were seated on the brick ledge. "You are never wrong. But this time you are not right."

My sap has frozen in my veins and my leaves have ceased their dance! Is it possible that these children question my wisdom? Keep still!

Now all is still—the breeze, my leaves… but the children?

The children looked about them, their hostile expressions now a little uncertain.

It was Pinky who piped up, "I like Saramma. She is like my mama. But my mama is not stupid."

The stillness persisted.

"We love you, Glate Peepal Thlee," Leena lisped. "But Thallamma knew the clow wath wicked."

"Yes," chimed in Deepa. "She would have known not to put him in the pantry."

The leaves suddenly rippled and danced. Was there a hint of laughter there? More stillness. Then:

I am the Great Peepal tree. I told you a true story.

The children were silent, deep in thought. Then Deepa spoke again, "The story is true according to before, like yesterday. But the story has to change today, and tomorrow it will be different. It is as you said, the times are changing."

The leaves were dancing again. The Great Peepal tree's branches swayed in the wind, and if its trunk could smile, it would have.

The children were less tense too.

Well, then children. Give me your version of the story when you come here tomorrow.

The children agreed and ran home again, for their mother was calling them to drink their evening glass of milk.

--

Deepa's Song of Saramma

Saramma, the sparrow, toiled tireless through the day.
She gathered golden grain, and stored them all away.
Morning after morning, Saramma worked the field,
Brimming up her storage urn with the summer yield.

Perched above, Crow sneered, "Why toil on a day so hot?
Such hard work, you silly bird, will profit you naught."
"Join me," called Saramma, "to feed you in your need.
When grey days come you will rue, you'll be sad indeed."

Crow took flight. His raucous laughter rang in her ears.
Saramma returned to work, eyes saddened by tears.
The monsoon clouds would herald only wind and rain;
No food for her babies – just misery and pain.

Carefully she stocked her urn then secured her door,
Shutting out rude cousin Crow, to think of him no more.
Tiny but tough, her brood's comfort she would ensure.
Lightning danced, thunder clapped, the sky began to pour.

Howling wind, lashing rain – fearsome was their battle.
The door to her dwelling began to shiver and rattle.
"Saramma, Saramma, I am drenched, let me in.
Saramma, Saramma, it's me, Crow, your cousin!"

"Go away Crow," she called, "I have no room for you,
You played all summer long, now in the rain you rue!"
"Saramma, don't be cruel, Saramma, pretty dear.
I'll nap in your pantry; with dawn I'll fly, don't fear!"

No trust had Saramma in her smooth-talking kin,
She hardened her heart, resolved to not let him in.
He could swear, he could shout, but for her babies' win,
She remained undeterred by Crow's unpleasant din.

Throughout that rainy night, Saramma stayed alert,
Her babies slept, she prepared mishap to avert.
When dawn broke her eyes were closed, tired from the vigil,
Her brood awoke and hungrily did chirp and trill.

"Wake up Ma, wake up. We want to eat," chirped the brood.
Saramma jumped and quickly viewed her stock of food,
She dipped into the urn, her hand held golden grain.
The babies fed, laughed with joy. Crow knew only rain.

Although the Great Peepal tree kept silent for many a day after that, the leaves continued to dance in the wind and ripple with laughter.

Chapter 4
Winter: The Grand Pumpkin

Ah children, come. It is many days since I have seen you last. I suppose the rains kept you indoors. But look now, the rushing river has subsided in its winding gorge, no longer snatching up animals, branches, even trees, to throw them downstream.

And see, the sun is shining in a warm, pleasant way. Many of my leaves have fallen this season, but the sunshine filters through my branches and can still warm you, although the breeze is cool.

The next harvest season is not far away, and you will be a year older than when you first came to this town. Your parents are seeking to move to a city where you can get a good education. Yes children, I see you are growing up. Deepa speaks with such wisdom and Leena lisps a little less. And little Pinky… no, no. Little Mohit. Little Mohit is grown up enough to insist we use his real name, although his cheeks are still pink.

Ah, I am just joking with you. I will miss you when you are gone. You have taught me that there is much to be learnt from children. But before we say goodbye, I want to tell you one more story. I want it to put a smile on your faces, and maybe cause you to laugh when you retell it to each other on a cold winter night as you snuggle in your blankets. It is the story of a grand pumpkin.

Subamma, an old woman, constantly complained. "What, no breakfast? There is never enough to eat in this house," she grumbled, glaring at her daughter-in-law. "My stomach is always noisy for want of food. No breakfast! How will I live?"

Daughter-in-law sighed. It was true. Her husband's earnings as a coolie stretched only so far. And this particular morning there was nothing to eat. While her husband and ample-bodied mother-in-law got a full plate of food almost every day, she herself was not so lucky.

"I want to eat well, this winter," Subamma said loudly. "So I will go visit my daughter who lives up the hill."

Subamma would have been happy had her daughter-in-law tried to stop her. But the calm lady with her gentle voice agreed. "You are right, Ma. You should visit my sister-in-law. It will make her very happy to see you."

Subamma continued to glare angrily. "I know, I know you wicked woman. You will be happy to see me go. You think I eat too much, don't you?"

With a loud snort, she grabbed up her shawl and staff and marched out of the house in a huff. Daughter-in-law followed her into the courtyard and handed her a clay canister full of water. Subamma snatched it from her and turned around to walk towards the hill, taking the support of her sturdy staff. She slowed a little as the trail turned uphill.

Daughter-in-law watched from afar till the plump old woman was lost to sight in the lush green of the forested hill. Then, with a sigh, she returned to her homely duties.

Subamma trudged uphill. The forest was thick on both sides of the narrow, winding trail. As she walked, her stomach rumbled yet again. *I wish I had something to eat,* she thought. She looked to either side as she walked, hoping to find some wild berries. Soon enough, she spied the dark red sour berries of the season amongst the thorned thickets. My daughter will love these, she exclaimed to herself and stepped off the trail to pick the berries. She picked plenty of them and knotted them in her handkerchief. But the thorns had torn her flesh and there was blood on her hands. When she turned around, she saw a great black wolf eying her. He had smelt her blood. The wolf bared his teeth and with a snarl said, "Aha, a meal! Come here, woman for I will now eat you!"

Subamma was frightened, but her mind began to whirr. "Of course, great wolf," she replied, the hint of a quiver in her voice. "But look at me; I am so thin. How can you enjoy this meal?" The wolf looked at her in surprise. *She is plump,* he thought.

Subamma continued, "I am going to my daughter who lives up the hill. She will feed me well. I will eat and drink there and become fat, then on my way back you can eat me."

The wolf liked the deal. "Okay, then. I will be waiting for you here. Do not think you can trick me," he warned.

"Oh, great wolf," said Subamma bowing humbly to him. "I will keep my promise. I will meet you here." The wolf stepped aside and allowed Subamma to get back on the trail.

Hurrying from the berry thickets, Subamma continued her journey. After some time, she found a boulder where she sat to sip water from her canister. As she cast her eyes around her, she spotted a deep purple stone-fruit on the ground. She walked over to it and saw more such fruit. She looked up to see that she had been sitting near a tall *jamun* tree. Delighted, she jumped up and began gathering *jamun* fruit from the ground to knot at the free end of her saree. Her daughter would love them.

As she was gathering the purple fruit, she heard a sudden rustle. She looked about her but could see no living being. The rustle came again. She looked up towards the sound then froze in fright. Draped lazily over a thick branch of the *jamun* tree, was a giant python. Swaying its tail, its scales gleaming in the sunlight that filtered through the canopy of the forest, the python was easily four times her own size. Flustered, Subamma stuttered, "Uh, uh, I am just going. L-leaving, r-right now."

The python hissed, "Tell me why I should not eat you. You came off your trail into my part of the jungle. This is my ssspace. I can eat you now and no one will quessstion me."

Subamma trembled. "Oh, glorious snake, I am on the way to my daughter's house up the hill. What a sorry meal I would make for you now. But my daughter will feed me well and when I return, I will be fat. If you want to eat me, wait till I come back. Then you will enjoy me as a meal."

The python hissed in laughter. "Old woman, you are clever. But I have just finished a big meal of a bandicoot and I am not hungry now. Hmmm, I think I will enjoy eating a fat woman so I will wait for you here on your return journey. Now get back to your trail thisss inssstance."

Subamma scrambled quickly back to the trail, beads of perspiration on her forehead. *That was close,* she thought then hastily continued up the trail towards her daughter's house.

She trudged onwards, leaning heavily on her staff. Her pace had slowed. She was tired and thirsty and her canister was now empty. Then, like music to her ears, she heard the distant sound of a rushing stream. *It must be this way,* she thought clambering off the trail once again following the sound of the water. Suddenly, there she saw it before her – a stream of water sparkling in the sunshine, playing music with its laughter as it tripped and fell over white stones.

Subamma was delighted and hurried towards the pretty sight before her. She dipped her hands and feet in the cool water and drank her fill. Then she held the canister down to let the water flow in. In that instant, in the tall green grass across the stream, she glimpsed a ripple of yellow and black. Subamma's blood ran cold. She looked up slowly into a pair of burning orange eyes. The majestic tiger before her made a guttural chuffing sound and Subamma's insides curled in fear. *I cannot get away this time,* she thought in panic.

"What are you doing at my watering hole?" the tiger demanded in his mighty, booming voice. Far and near, big and small, all the forest animals trembled at the sound.

Subamma blabbered in fright. Then her presence of mind kicked in. "Oh, Tiger, your majesty," she said bowing low. "I am going to my daughter's house up the hill, but I am so thirsty. I came to fill my canister."

The tiger continued to watch her through narrowed eyes, his colors glowing, his muscles tense.

"Don't... Don't eat me now. When I return from my daughter's place, I will be fat and fine, and you can eat me on my way back down the hill, Subamma offered desperately.

The tiger drawled out a guttural "Hmmm."

"I promise," Subamma added, panic rising in her voice.

"Woman," the tiger thundered. "I don't kill at my watering hole. But since you promise, I will eat you on your way back."

Subamma wasn't sure but was that tiger hiding a smile? She dared not move.

The tiger continued, "Do not try to deceive me, or it will not go well for you. Now go!"

His sinister snarl sent Subamma scrambling back onto the trail. It was the first time that saucy Subamma had ever felt real, deep fear. From then on, she stayed firmly on the road looking neither right nor left. By nightfall, she was sitting in her beloved daughter's home before a delicious dinner spread.

When she awoke the next morning, Subamma noted how her daughter's house was bright and well-kept inside and was surrounded by fields of vegetables, grain and lentils, which her farmer son-in-law tended to. Over the next two months, she ate her fill of all the fresh greens that were brought to the house and everything else that her daughter cooked. Indeed, Subamma was having the best time of her life. She ate and ate and ate until she was no longer plump. She caught her reflection in the mirror; she had actually become fat!

Then the day came when she began to think of returning to her son's house. No matter how saucily she spoke to her daughter-in-law, she really missed her kindness and gentle words, although she was not about to tell her so. But how would Subamma return?

The tiger will certainly stalk me, she thought, *I stand no chance. But if somehow, I do escape him, there is the snake still lying in wait for me. The python has only to slip off the branch above to crush me with her weight. If, by chance, that*

*doesn't happen and I escape her slippery coils, I would still
have to outrun the great black wolf!*

Subamma ate and she thought and she thought and she ate.
Finally, a plan began to take shape in her mind.

She told her daughter, "I will go back to your brother's
house tomorrow. But I need to take home a gift from you."

"Ma, anything you want," said her faithful daughter. Her
son-in-law echoed the sentiment.

"Can you give me a pumpkin? The biggest pumpkin you
have in your field? The biggest, biggest that you can find? As
big as me?"

To her delight, son-in-law actually brought home a
pumpkin almost as big as her. Under Subamma's watchful
eye, he scooped out the inside. As Subamma meant to ride the
pumpkin home, a slit was made at the front of the hollow
pumpkin to give her a clear view ahead. Two wooden wheels
were fitted on both sides with pedals inside to work them. And
at Subamma's request, a small hole was made at the back, and
just below it was fixed an earthen basin, which she directed
her daughter to heap up with the ash from her stove.

"But Ma, what is the ash for? And how will you use it
when you would be pedaling with both hands?" her daughter
asked.

"Don't you worry," said Subamma with a wicked gleam
in her eye. "I know what to do with the ash and how to do it."

Next morning, her daughter waved goodbye as Subamma
set off in her pumpkin, downhill on the forest trail.

The pumpkin entered the forest and rolled along until the
sound of the bubbling stream came to Subamma's ear. This
was the tiger's territory, she knew.

Sure enough; the majestic tiger caught sight of the rolling orange pumpkin and, filled with curiosity, bounded after it. There was a familiar smell about it… a smell like the woman at his watering hole, he recalled. On a hunch, he growled, "Woman, I know you are here. Come out as you promised so that I can eat you!"

Subamma immediately pedaled harder and shouted, "*Chal mere kaddu, tarum-turum.* Roll my Pumpkin, *tarum-turum*!"

With that, she let out a big blast of wind from her behind. The force of her wind caught up the ash in the basin and it flew out behind the pumpkin straight into the eyes of the tiger. The tiger stopped in his tracks as the ash stung his eyes. He began shaking his great head in pain and roared loudly. "And what is this terrible smell?"

Blinded by the ash and very unhappy, the tiger could no longer keep up with the pumpkin. He trailed back to his watering hole to wash his eyes and the dreadful smell from his nose.

Subamma pedaled steadily on until she came upon the tall *jamun* tree. Through the slit in the pumpkin, she could see the immense python draped on a thick branch overhanging the forest trail. She stayed slow and steady until just before she reached that branch, then with a spurt of speed pedaled as fast as she could for her life depended on it. As she passed the branch, the large, heavy python dropped her weight aiming to land on the moving pumpkin. She missed by a few inches and hit the forest ground instead.

Clear of the python, Subamma let out another blast of wind from her behind and ash flew into the python's eyes, and mouth covering its slippery, forked tongue. "Eew, what an awful sssmell," the snake exclaimed.

"Chal mere kaddu, tarum-turum. Roll my Pumpkin, *tarum-turum!"* shouted Subamma with glee. By the time the python recovered from the reek of the blast of ash, Subamma was far ahead and the sluggish snake had no heart to slither after her.

Still pedaling, Subamma approached the thorny thicket of jungle berries. The great wolf, who was hanging out there, was surprised to see a rolling pumpkin. "Wait, great pumpkin," he shouted. "Have you seen an old woman coming downhill?"

The pumpkin silently rolled on. The wolf sniffed the air and now smelt something familiar. "You smell like the old woman. Show yourself, old woman," he commanded.

Subamma cackled with laughter inside her pumpkin. She had already fooled a tiger, and a python. "I will not stop until I get to my son's house. And no, you cannot eat me," she shouted happily to the wolf. *"Chal mere kaddu, tarum-turum!"*

She sped ahead spewing stinking ash into the wolf's face. Confused and disoriented, the wolf hit his head on a tree and fell. In a daze, he watched the grand orange pumpkin roll downhill.

Soon, Subamma was out of the jungle and at the foot of the hill, she could clearly see her son's cottage ahead. She rolled her pumpkin to a halt in her son's courtyard. She stepped out of her orange carriage beaming from ear to ear, as her son and daughter-in-law looked on in amazement.

"What a huge pumpkin, Mama," her son said in admiration.

Subamma grinned. It was a happy day.

"Your sister sent it for my daughter-in-law," she said actually smiling. Daughter-in-law looked at her in wonder. "We can eat the pumpkin for many months," Subamma added.

"But Mama, why do you smell so bad?" her son asked.

She laughed long and hard. Finally, she said, "Oh, I have to visit the toilet, and then I need a bath." She ran towards the bathroom.

Afterwards, daughter-in-law called her for dinner. From her cozy bed, happy Subamma replied sleepily, "No, not tonight. I'm full. You both eat."

------------------- The End --------------------